Hugo's Hullabaloo

Ed Boxall

WALKER BOOKS
AND SUBSIDIARIES

LONDON · BOSTON · SYDNEY · AUCKLAND

There was once a King and Queen.
They lived in a big, big castle.

The King and Queen had a son.
He was called Prince Hugo.

When Prince Hugo was five,
the King and Queen built him
a school in the castle.
He was the only pupil. He could
choose whatever lessons he liked.

Monday	Tuesday	Wednesday
daydreaming	resting	ice-cream-eating
resting	ice-cream-eating	storytime
ice-cream-eating	storytime	watching TV
storytime	watching TV	daydreaming
watching TV	daydreaming	resting

minty choc
and plum

starfish
and jam

Honey and
chestnut

Friday

rsday	Friday
me	ice-cream-eating
ing TV	resting
reaming	watching TV
ing	daydreaming
e-cream-eating	storytime

Ice cream Flavours

minty choc
and plum $\frac{8}{10}$

Starfish
and jam $\frac{0}{10}$

Honey and
chestnut $\frac{10}{10}$

The King and Queen ordered lots of people to look after Prince Hugo.

He had someone to scratch his itches.

Someone to blow his nose.

Someone to trim his toenails.

Someone to
cut his hair.

And
someone
to get the
wax out of
his ears.

The King and Queen gave Prince Hugo
lots of presents. On his sixth birthday
they gave him 365 pairs of trainers:
one pair for every day of the year.

"Thank you," said Hugo politely.

On his seventh birthday they gave him his own bowling alley. It had fifteen lanes.

HUGO

Happy
Birthday
Hugo

"Thank you," said Hugo politely.

On his eighth birthday they gave him his own fairground.
The rollercoaster was bigger than the one in Disneyland.

"Thank you," said Hugo politely.

Weeks passed.
The bowling alley was covered with dust.
Months passed.
The fairground was covered with cobwebs.

Every day Prince Hugo sat at the top
of the castle and looked out at the
children playing in the village.

"Something is wrong," said the King. "Something is very wrong," said the Queen.

All he does is stare out of the window with a face like a droopy geranium.

My goodness! He's been wearing the same pair of trainers for a week!

So the King and Queen called
the best doctors in the land.
"Find out what is wrong
with Prince Hugo!"
they begged.

Loneliobolitus

The first doctor pushed
and prodded him.

Maybeabitlonelicus

The second
doctor prodded
and poked him.

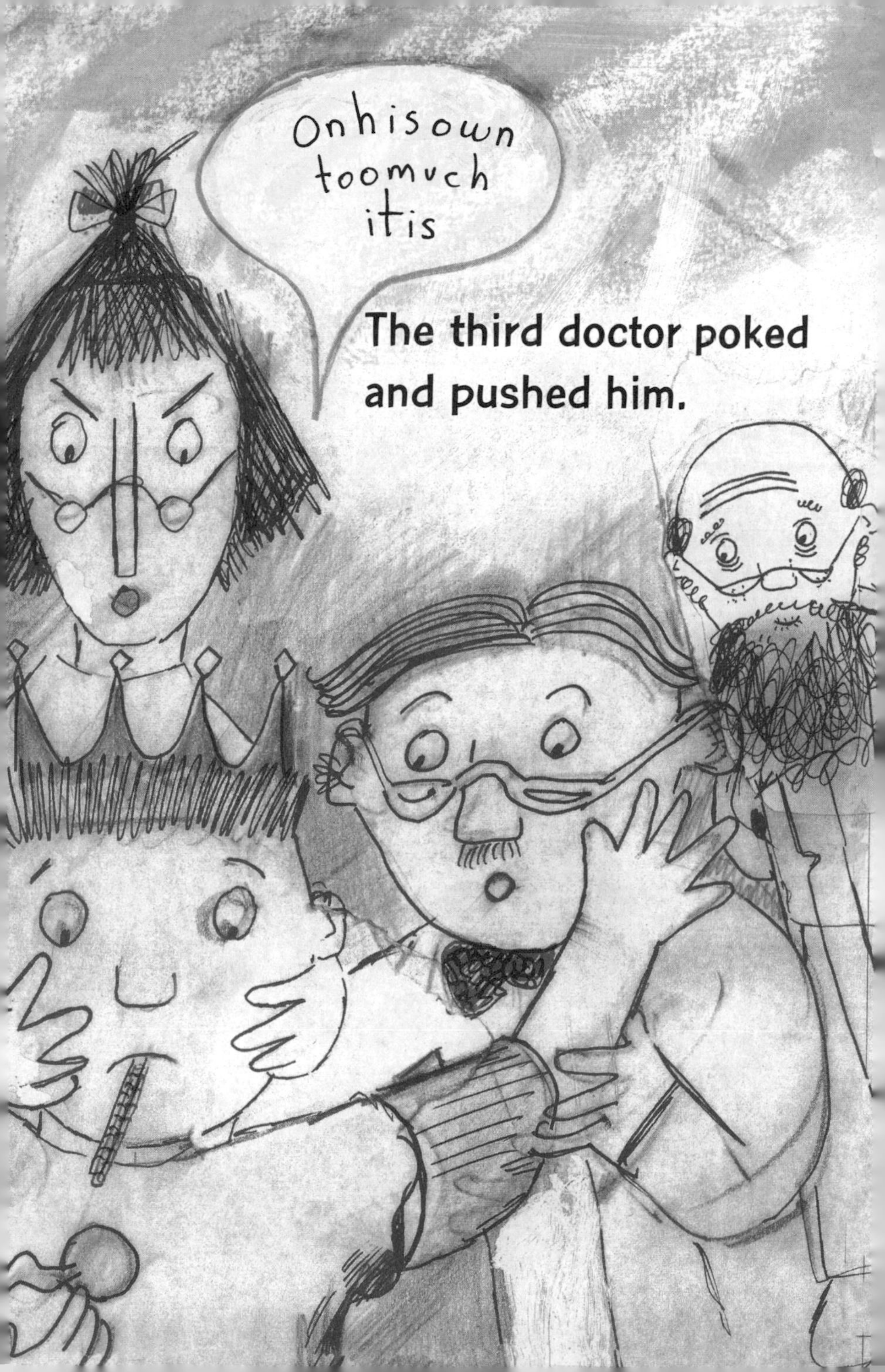

The third doctor poked and pushed him.

The King and Queen were puzzled.
Then the fourth doctor (he was the
oldest and wisest) said quietly,
"When was the last time he had a
wild hullabaloo with his friends?"

The King and Queen were more puzzled.

The wise old doctor wrote out a
prescription.

PRESCRIPTION

For persistent loneliness:

ONE SURPRISE
HULLABALOO

Dr V.V. Wise

Every child from the
village <u>must</u> be invited

The Queen gasped when she read it.
The King fainted when he read it.
"Oh no! We don't want him playing
with the village children!" they said.

But they DID want their son to be happy.
So the King and Queen spent all day writing invitations.

This is what they wrote:

Dear Village Child
Please come to Prince Hugo's

Surprise Hullabaloo

On 23rd September
At the big castle
From 9 a.m. till whenever.

The King and Queen

PS Please have a bath before you come.
PPS Please clean your teeth.
PPPS Please try not to break anything.
PPPPS Please don't tell Prince Hugo –
  it's a SURPRISE!

They sent an invitation to
every child in the village.

Cool!

Woof!

Excellent!

Brilliant!

Hooray! Hooray!
Meeow! Meeow!

Prince Hugo sat at his window.
He felt more lonely than ever.

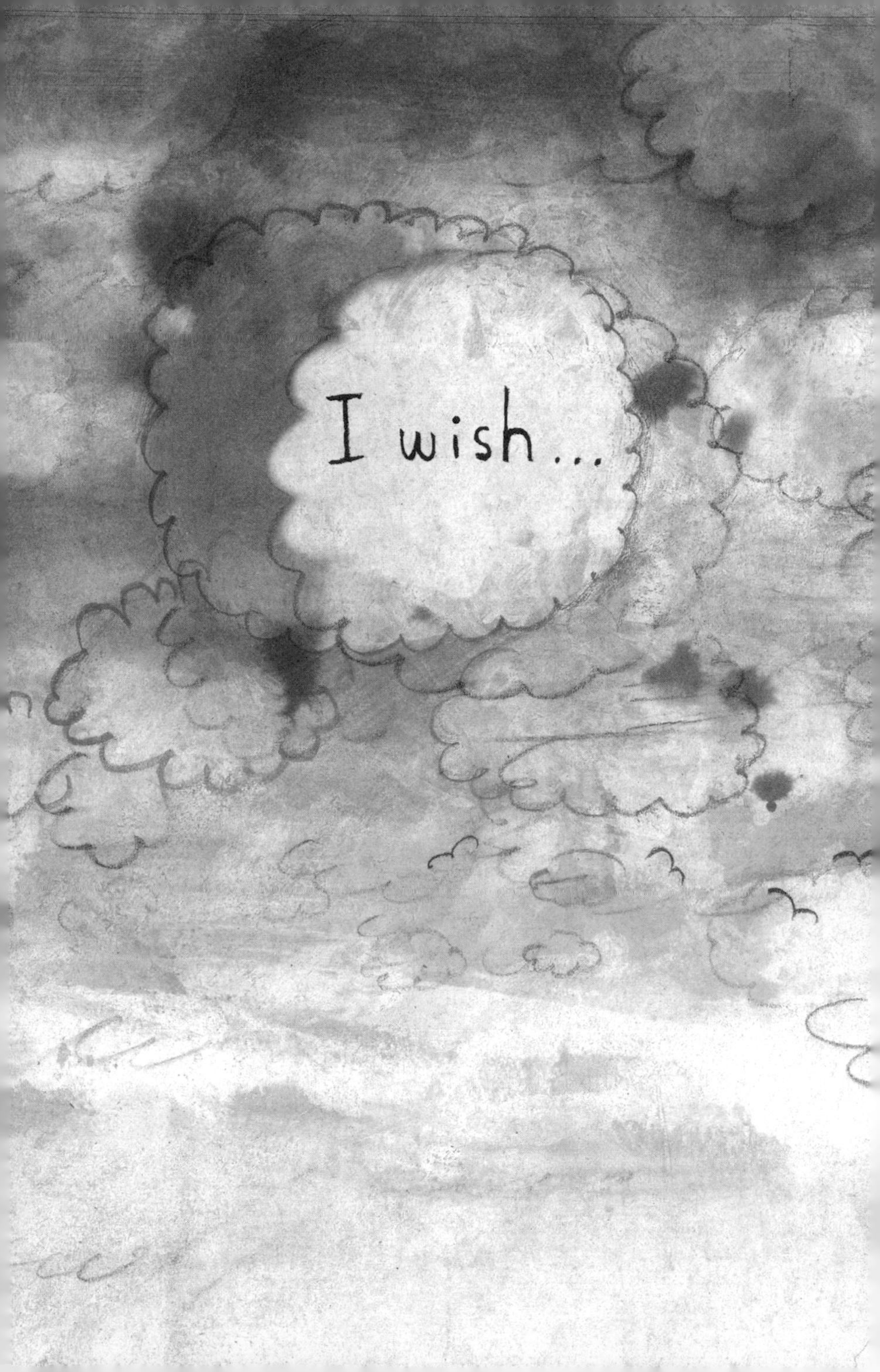
I wish...

By 7a.m. on party day the children were outside the castle gates with their mums and dads.

At 9a.m. the gates were opened.
The crowd gasped at the sight
of the enormous castle.

Everyone bowed when they walked past the King and Queen.

You know... their teeth look quite clean.

And they don't smell like old cabbage at all.

Everyone waited nervously for the Prince. "SURPRISE!" they shouted when he came out of the castle door.

At first the children were shy, but before long they were running and playing all round the castle. Prince Hugo joined in. The children soon forgot he was special.

And Hugo forgot he was a prince.

When the King and Queen saw
how happy he was, they jumped
on the rollercoaster and
joined in the fun.

All too soon (and long past everyone's bedtime), it was time to say goodbye. "Thank you for a great hullabaloo," the children said to Prince Hugo. "Thank you for a great hullabaloo," Prince Hugo said to his mum and dad.

"Thank you for a great idea," the King and Queen said to the wise old doctor.

From that day on Prince Hugo went to school in the village.

After school he was allowed to play
with his new friends — as long as he
was home by six o'clock and didn't
have any homework.

And every weekend the fairground
and bowling alley were opened up
so that everyone could enjoy them.

On Hugo's ninth birthday the King
and Queen bought rollerblades
for EVERYONE!

For My Family
E.B.

First published 2004 by Walker Books Ltd
87 Vauxhall Walk, London SE11 5HJ

2 4 6 8 10 9 7 5 3 1

Text and illustrations © 2004 Ed Boxall

The right of Ed Boxall to be identified as author/illustrator of this work
has been asserted by him in accordance with the Copyright, Designs
and Patents Act 1988

This book has been typeset in Contemporary Brush-Bold

Handlettering by Ed Boxall

Printed in China

British Library Cataloguing in Publication Data:
a catalogue record for this book
is available from the British Library

ISBN 1-84428-639-8

www.walkerbooks.co.uk